T0064175

The WILL Of GOD

The WILL OF GOD

SEEMA SUDAN

PARTRIDGE

Print information available on the last page.

To order additional copies of this book, contact
Partridge India
000 800 919 0634 (Call Free)
+91 000 80091 90634 (Outside India)
orders.india@partridgepublishing.com

www.partridgepublishing.com/india

DEDICATION

To my father in law, late Shri H.C Chaudhry.

Acknowledgements

This book was a dream, the idea of which has been shaped by several hundred people from across the world. I would like to thank them all in general and in particular:

Ekta Kapoor: The original drama queen of the Indian soap opera whose success gave flight to my own creative imagination.

Deepak Chaudhry: My husband and soulmate, for giving me the strength to follow my dream.

Savita and Narinder Sudan: My parents, for their constant support and guidance. Krishna Chaudhry: My mother-in-law, for her understanding.

Mrs Rachana Pant: My high school English teacher, for introducing me to the wonderful world of words and their magical creativity.

The Editor and the entire team of Partridge India for being so efficient and professional throughout the publishing process.

Shobha Sengupta: For editing

Shyamal Banerjee for giving the cover painting. Last but not the least, my twins Ria and Rohan who gave me a new direction in life.

ABOUT THE AUTHOR

Seema Sudan Chaudhry was born and brought up in Delhi. She graduated in history from Lady Shri Ram College. Seema got interested in writing while a freshman at high school, when she published her first article and went on to win the 'insight'-creative writing competition at the university level. The author is also, a sports enthusiast, a Delhi state level player in badminton.

Although she joined her family business and travelled all over the world, gaining rich cross cultural experience, her heart was always in pursuing a career in writing. Now twenty years later she has found her true calling in writing. Though she has written columns for magazines, this book is her first novella.

CHAPTER 1

As she searched the faces of those around the table for remorse or sympathy, she could find neither. In a room full of family and friends, she could not see a single soul who genuinely cared for her. Seated right next was her husband , Raj. Ten years had changed him so much, she thought, he was the most agitated as her actions had harmed him the most, thinning the smooth supply of money for his party. Next to him were seated her equally agitated brothers. My brothers…ha, ha… she thought, how smoothly and conveniently they had taken over the role of spectators, looking and passing judgement on her, making sure that she walked the straight line set for her to walk on, which she did to perfection, but in complete ignorance. Next to them, was seated her friend, Meera, friends for thirty years, my God how could I not see through her earlier, she seemed the most comfortably, uncomfortable, she had made sure she had a safe haven.

And last but not the least, was the business head of the mammoth conglomerate, which was to set base here, had things gone according to their plan. His agitation matched that of her husband, the only difference, colour of bloodshot red eyes by a few degrees. Chris, had started exploring and expanding his business ventures into India in early 1999. His business was spread vastly in two major fields of work, commodities and real estate. He had foreseen the impending instability that would follow in his own country and was convinced that India was the right place to invest and keep the ball rolling.

My God, she thought, if I ever get out of this, how can I carry on with them. The thought revolted her and brought on a feeling of nausea that almost made her faint. "Are you alright madam? Should we send for a doctor?" Asked the office boy, the only one who noticed her discomfort in the room. "She's alright, get out" came the tart reply from the seat next to her.

She decided it was time to open up the discussion. "Sometimes, it's the will of God". Everyone in the room looked at her as she spoke these words. The expressions on their faces reflected disbelief and despair, and as she looked at each one of them, she decided to keep her mouth shut, at least for the time being.

Not far from there, just fifteen kilometres away, there was another meeting was going on. Sitting in it was Rohan, a small time businessman. To the right of Rohan sat his wife Deepa. To his left, sat his mother and directly opposite him was a white faced Egyptian. The Egyptian looked as if he had just seen a ghost, his otherwise red glowing face looked completely ashen, but with a hint of a bewildered smile at one corner of his mouth as if he was deciding, whether the news that was just delivered to him was the good part of the bad or bad part of the good. The sheer similarity of expression on their faces was that of stark disbelief. Rohan decided someone had to take charge and as he spoke he heard his voice without actually feeling the words leave his mouth. "It's the will of God… I guess." As soon as he said that, he felt all three set of eyes staring at him, and decided to keep quiet for the rest of the meeting. However, the euphoria that was building inside of him was hard to contain as he smiled the most fantastic smile, and looked up and said to himself, "Thank you God, now I know you still exist." As if taking the queue from him everyone on the table started smiling, slyly at first and then openly. They all knew that they had finally won.

It all started six weeks ago, with the devastatingly matter of fact letter from the bank, the Uppals were a prosperous and respected family, they were held as an example of inspiring entrepreneurship. The family had started their textile garment export unit fifteen years back and already were on the way to making their name as one of the leading exporters in the capital city, Delhi. As prosperity came many varied investments were made, some good, some bad, though they were well prepared for the recession in the global market or so they thought, as most of us do. The Uppal did not believe that the golden sun shining on them would ever set. That is why the bank letter was such a shock, especially after the reassurance from the top bank management, that whatever may happen, the bank would support them, as they had been one of the most loyal customers. It was on this assurance that Senior Uppal, Rohan's father had submitted all his properties to the bank as collateral in exchange for their continued support to the now ever decreasing list of orders.

As the senior Uppal stood still, very still, letting the impact of what this meant for him and his family, the first thought that hit him was - they told me, they all told me never to trust a banker, but how could he, after all these years. We were like partners, brothers, he shared my profits, he has no conscience at all????? What have I done? And my son what will he say, he told me not to do this, I should have listened to him, no, there is a mistake somewhere, this cannot happen, it cannot end like this, and at that he burst out laughing, laughing a strange laugh of pain and anguish.

So strange was the booming sound of that laugh that the palatial house resounded with its echo, and brought all the family members to the source of it. As the three of them reached him, senior Uppal was still in a state of shock laughing madly with tears streaming down his face. His wife was the first to reach him she shook him, wildly, he collapsed, right there in her arms.

The youngest Uppal, Samir was the first to react, as he screamed "get him to a hospital". The next hour was a mad frenzy, as their car tried to make its way to the hospital only about two blocks away, but the mad morning traffic was taking away precious seconds. As they screeched to a halt at the emergency gate, the medical team was ready and Rohan thought, thank God; his wife had called and alerted them.

As the medics took over, the two brothers were left outside the ICU, to wait, till the doctors informed them of the situation. As they both sat down, they looked at each other, asking the same question "what happened???"

The door burst open as their mother and Deepa entered, half walking and half running. They were all anxious, but reassured one another. Deepa looked at Rohan and bid him to come to a side, as she wanted to say something. As soon as they were alone she handed him the letter from the bank, and spoke in a whisper barely loud enough for Rohan to hear......

"I found it on the chair papa was sitting on, I think, you better take a look at it".

As Rohan read the contents of the letter, his face grew very still, his expression not showing any emotions. He quietly folded and pocketed it, he looked at Deepa squarely and said "Not a word right now, now is not the time". He then went back to the ICU to find out what was happening inside.

Six hours later, as the door to the operation theatre opened and doctors and nurses started walking out, the family rushed towards them, as they reached the surgeon, they searched his face for clues, the question on the tip of their tongues, but no words came out. The surgeon's face relaxed, as he informed them that their father was going to make it. "He will not be the same in his physical capabilities but he will make it none the less". Then after a seconds' hesitation, he added "It will take a lot of time and patience but with therapy, slowly he will get much better". Having informed them the surgeon quickly moved on, to catch up with his colleagues.

Once they heard the good news they relaxed. As they started to move towards the benches, Rohan decided, it was time to talk, as time was of the essence. He looked around and walked up to the nurses. "Sister, he spoke with slight hesitation. "My wife will be here, if you need anything, do let her know". With that, Rohan walked towards the admission counter in order to complete all the paper work required. With all the necessary formalities over, Rohan called his mother and Samir aside. As soon as they were out of the audible range of the small crowed present at the entrance, Rohan started to speak. "This is not a good time to discuss business but, papa, it seems, received a letter from the bank. They have issued a notice of recovery against our company and have given us forty five days to pay up all outstanding dues. Samir looked completely baffled, "How is that possible, we just received the biggest order of the season, they have to service it, damn blast it." Exploded Samir. "He promised us, even took a big advance on his share of the profit, that insect, I will report him, his career will be over, he doesn't know me….". Rohan looked at him and added quietly. "He, it seems, Samir, was promoted to the post of General Manager, that is what he is now."

Early next morning both brothers sat down to decide what course of action will have to be taken, Samir seemed nervous when he asked his brother. "What can we do now, I have to tell my in–laws". Samir had been engaged to his long time sweetheart and they were to be married at the end of the month. The girl, Natasha, belonged to a very prosperous Punjabi family. They owned one of the oldest business houses in the city. Rohan took a deep breath before he spoke, "Look Samir, we need all the help we can get, or the consequences are not very good. We have this house, thank God, but the rest is all mortgaged. We still need to complete the order at hand, we need another 3000 tonne of rice. Now with no support from the bank, I do not know how we will achieve that. We will have to find other means". Suddenly he stopped, and looked at Samir with a completely exasperated expression on his face," What I am trying to say brother is, that we stick together now more than ever." Rohan looked directly into his brother's eyes, "Yes" came a nervous reply from Samir.

It sounded weak, as if the word was forced out of him. I must be mistaken thought Rohan to himself.

As both brothers left for the day's work, a very scared and nervous Deepa was left alone. Deepa was not particularly a religious person but at a time like this it seemed the most natural thing to do and she folded her hands in prayer. The senior Mrs Uppal sitting in the hospital had just done exactly the same. In lord we trust, please forgive our follies and mistakes and, carry us out of, this time of difficulty, she prayed fervently.

CHAPTER 2

Rohan had no other interest, besides his work. His passion for his business was almost to the extent of an obsession. Having seen his father and mother struggle, he had very early in life become involved in work. By the time he graduated, he was heading two units involved in exports of garments to Europe. The boom in exports and the never ending shipment deadlines kept him away from most of the social events with family and friends. The time that he did not spend in his office, was spent in his travels to Europe. Although he was very satisfied with his social life or the complete lack of it, it was only after he met Deepa that he began to yearn for more and more time off from work.

Initially it had been taking a few hours off to meet her, but gradually as they began to get closer to each other, Rohan started to take more and more time off from work. His family had started to suspect something when he took his Sundays off. The first one everyone remembered and still talked about. Deepa had been very busy throughout the week and could only manage to make time on a Sunday, so Rohan decided to take off and spend their Sunday together. As they sat on the biggest and the most secluded rock they could find in the beautiful surroundings of the legendary gardens, they talked and held hands looking deep into each others eyes. Completely love struck, and oblivious to all those who bothered to watch them. It was at that moment, that Rohan's mobile started to buzz, Deepa still broke into an uncontrollable bout of laugh, whenever she talked about it. "The first call was from his mama, and he went yes,

yes, yes........ I am alright, no mom, I am ok just decided to take a Sunday off" she would go on in between bouts of laughter. "Then the second call was from his dad, Just to confirm if what his wife told him was the truth, they kept calling every ten minutes or so to see if he was feeling all right, even two supervisors from the shop floor of the factory called up", and then she invariably burst out laughing, unable to go on.

As they got closer and in a more serious relationship, the Sundays off for Rohan soon became an accepted fact, his parents were actually glad that Rohan was starting to socialise more. It was only when Sundays gave way to weekends off for Rohan, that everyone started to wonder.

The most perturbed was his mother, who was fiercely possessive of her sons, she was the first to guess that it had to be the doing of some 'female element' that was distracting her first born not only from work but also from his family. Whenever she walked into Rohan's office unannounced, she would either see him grinning at nothing at all, or he would be on the phone and would quickly end the conversation.

Finally, his parents confronted him, it was then that he introduced Deepa to his family. The wedding took place the following spring. It was the most beautiful spring of Deepa's life as Rohan swept her off her feet with love and tenderness. Life was perfect, well, almost. The only small glitch in the way of perfection was the fact that Deepa's mother-in law though she had welcomed her with open arms but there was an undertone of resentment towards her. Which started to show in comical ways, one such episode was on the dining table. Every night as the family sat down to dine, Deepa invariably found her mother-in law sitting between her and Rohan. Soon the comedy took on biblical proportions, as Deepa started to nudge her way to the seat next to her husband. As the cold war continued between the two the rest of the family enjoyed dinner oblivious to it. "She started playing dirty, she would ask me to pass her something from the kitchen, and when I got back, there she would be sitting on my seat. It was so annoying ". Deepa would confide to her closest friend.

It was on the day that Samir, the younger son, introduced Natasha to his family that the Senior Mrs Uppal gave in. Her focus shifted to the younger one and his love interest. Deepa, finally, after a year of marriage, took her seat next to Rohan on the dining table, without anymore tricks from her mother-in-law, and the food suddenly started to taste so much better to her.

As time moved on, Deepa, became the pillar of strength for all of them, especially when the downturn started. She soon became indispensable, especially to her mother-in-law.

Rohan could think of little else to do at the moment, so he decided to go to the bank and meet Mr Sharma, their confidante and partner for many years, who had recently been promoted to the post of General Manager of the bank. Rohan entered the bank building and tried to get in touch with him, he was told politely, to take an appointment, as at that moment, the General Manager was in a meeting. With little else to do he fixed an appointment for the following day and decided to go back and check on work at office. As Rohan entered his office, he asked his secretary to update him on the rice deliveries at the port and the outstanding payments, which were to be made to the rice millers and agents. As he sat alone in his immaculate office he thought back....... the luxurious life that they had lived, in the not so distant past, how Samir had been pampered by. In fact Rohan had spoiled him the most, by giving in to all his demands. He had always been there for his little brother, even taking the responsibility for his misdoings on many an occasion. Rohan, being seven years elder to

Samir, had seen their father struggle hard to set up his own little business empire, he had seen his mother cutting corners, here and there, most often on things for herself. He himself had, had a very austere living. Often family and friends warned him of over indulgence towards his younger brother, which he waved off casually saying: "He has it, so let him flaunt it."

The last few years and especially the last few months had been extremely difficult though, as recession had been slowly taking away the orders in hand and even some of the orders for which the material was ready had been cancelled, readymade garments were piling up. Labour had been restless, with no work at hand. Effort to layoff had backfired. There had been violence and cases were piling up. There seemed to be pressure on all sides, Rohan had often thought in the last few months, "When it rains it pours".

At such a time getting an order for export of rice had appeared godsend, it seemed too good to be true, especially at the quoted price. The bank did have objections at first, as rice was not their, the Uppal's, primary field of work in export. However, after much haggling they had conceded to it, conditional, to putting up extra collateral security for hundred percent of the order value, which the senior Uppal had willingly agreed to. This was a trap laid by the bank for taking more security, a trap in which the Uppals would lose everything, as they had taken private loans to put up the margin for the purchase of rice stock. At this point the only option left was to take credit from the rice supplier. Which seemed impossible, as they were new to the rice trade, the only other way was to take private loans against the house, the only property they were left with now. As all these thoughts were welling up inside of him and his mind was in a state of complete turmoil. Suddenly, he was brought back to the present as the door was flung open, and a visibly happy Samir stood beaming. As Samir came up to him he gushed: "I am alright, you don't have to worry about me now!!!!!!"

"Huh, what?? what are you saying?", asked Rohan. "Oh! bhai (hey, brother), my in-laws, they are taking me on as their partner, so you don't have to worry about me, they only want me to resign here." He went on as if declaring his decision, Rohan heard him but could not immediately comprehend the implications of It, "I can look after dad in the hospital while you are busy" Samir added, as if to confirm to his brother, that what he heard was right.

Rohan stared at him, hearing him but not believing what he just heard. Then he thought: "Rats are the first to desert a sinking ship". It is my own fault, my brother has become a rat and he is deserting my sinking ship.

CHAPTER 3

In another office, sat the Chief Minister of Delhi-Taradevi. She was deep thought, as she reflected back on her life's journey.

Tara at eighteen years of age was a tall, slim girl, with pearly white complexion and a taut, well curved body. She had never enjoyed her father's attention as her brothers did. They were always closer to him, but her moments of pride came, whenever she scored well in her school, her father would shower praise on her. She always heard her father speak highly of people who were well educated especially people from around their village, who often came to her father for advice and financial assistance. "It was probably because of the fact that he himself was not well educated," she thought. He had barely passed his fifth standard in school when he joined the family business.

Their family was one of the oldest landlords in the state and prided themselves for having continued the tradition. Vastly popular and respected in the district and it was because of this influence that they commanded in the region, that many a political party tried to woo their support.

Despite the traditional values of the family, her father had supported her decision for higher studies. Even though her two brothers had joined business soon after their high school. In a way she felt she had become closer to her father now, as he started taking her advice on different issues outside of household. But it was that one day which changed everything and made her realise that when you are born in a distinguished traditional family, you have to pay the price for it, especially if you are born a girl.

It was a cool summer morning and as she walked out into the open, leaving the enclosed walls of her palatial house. She felt the cool grass underneath her bare feet. The lawns were recently trimmed,"Maybe today" she thought as the green grass tingled her beautifully manicured feet. As she strolled callously on the lawns around her house, raising her arms, and embracing herself, she felt a wonderful warmth rising inside of her, "This is the happiest day of my life" she thought to herself. She was in love, so completely in love and the man of her dreams had proposed to her for marriage. "I cannot wait for papa to get home, I know he will be proud of me when I tell him about Suraj." Suraj was the son of a principal, principal of the only school present between the five villages surrounding their estate.

The weather suddenly changed, as the winds picked up speed, Tara closed her eyes to enjoy the feel of it on her skin, as she took a whiff of the air and in doing so, she smelled the rain before it actually hit her. Her nostrils were filled with the wet muddy and beautifully welcome smell of the rain, as the drops of water fell on her skin they seemed to connect with and bring alive each and every sensation of her body. The nervousness of disclosing her secret to her father slowly started to melt away as wave after wave tingling droplets of water fell from the sky. She started to walk faster in order to reach the thick bunch of trees for shelter, but how much so ever fast she walked, the rain was faster and quicker. She walked a few paces, and then started to run feeling like a child trying to play with this magnificent downpour of mother nature. The shade of the tree under which she took shelter proved to be of not much use as the rain gathered more and more momentum. Giving up her efforts to hide from it she decided to befriend it and enjoy the experience. She stretched her arms to the point that her muscles and joints started to complain, turned her face up towards the sky, as if in an invitation to the rain and then slowly began to step out of her shelter. She stood with her eyes closed and arms stretched wide as she let the rain hit her full blast, it was a gesture of complete surrender of body and mind. As she let herself go, she felt tingling sensations erupt inside of her. Her skin started to glow as the rain washed over it endlessly, her mind was screaming , it wanted to sing, she wanted to dance, jump, shout all at once.

The blaring angry noise of honking suddenly brought her back to reality. As she looked in the direction from where the offending sound was coming, she saw her father, her very angry father blasting away the car horn. She suddenly realised she was standing in the middle of the driveway, "when did I reach here" she thought. As she shifted her gaze back to the car and started moving away apologetically, she saw a tall well groomed man sitting beside her father, as the car made its way towards the house, she saw him looking at her, " Was that a smile on his face, who is he???" she thought. That was her first meeting with Raj.

Tara walked out of her room only when she heard the roar of the car engine, " Oh good, the guest is leaving". As she walked into the family room, she was greeted by her mother, father and her elder brother. "Come Tara we have some news for you." 'Huh …what, what is it??" asked Tara. Her brother said "we just got a marriage proposal for you, the boy is the son of a local politician, you will be very happy." She looked at her father, who nodded in agreement, then at her mother, who was beaming with happiness. "You will live like a queen ", she said to Tara. "I..... eh.. I wanted to tell you all about Suraj. He............", She looked at their faces to see how they were reacting to her words. Her brother was glaring at her as if daring her to go on, and her mother looked as if she would start crying, she looked at Tara pleadingly. But it was her father who spoke with complete authority as he stood up "Tara, it is settled you are to be married to Raj Singh, I will set up the date about three months from now, that should give us enough time for all the preparations." He then moved towards the door, just as he was about to exit, he turned and added "forget about everything else, there is going to be no further discussion on it."

It was later at night that she took her mother in confidence and told her about Suraj. Her mother was shocked and warned her, and pleaded with her not to say a word of it to anyone, "Tara if you so much as mention this to anyone you will put yourself in a difficult situation and compromise Suraj as well as his family." With that her fate was sealed.

Her life changed dramatically after marriage, as the lady of the house and the wife of the Chief minister. She did her duty to perfection on both grounds. The test of her perseverance however, came during the trying time when Raj's name was listed as a suspect in the hawala money scam. Raj was denied a ticket to fight the elections, instead, she was pushed to the forefront, which she vehemently opposed, as she had conceived for the first time since her marriage to Raj and did not want to take any chances. She was cajoled, manipulated and pushed to the political forefront. As a result of all the stress, she had a miscarriage and lost her child. Her husband and brothers seized the opportunity and in the name of 'upliftment of women', won the elections with a clear majority. Three years in power had been exciting and exhilarating but now, at a personal level, she felt lonely and the inability to have children added to her loneliness. Raj was a good provider, even a good companion whenever he was around, which was becoming more and more rare. She was beginning to feel the loneliness and her want for a child was pushing her towards depression.

The depression was deepening and her concentration had started to dwindle, it was even more accentuated by the fact that no one else shared her concern.

As she now sat alone in her lavish office, she looked around. The room was huge and tastefully decorated yet simple, her teakwood table was the only magnificent piece of furniture. On the grey carpeted floor at the one end stood a cupboard full of and medals. As she she looked at them, the door opened and her secretary and friend of many years, Meera walked in "you look so glum, what is the matter? You have a meeting to attend in twenty minutes, followed by a press release. You need to cheer up."

"Yes, Meera, give me two minutes and I shall have my smile back on," replied Taradevi.

"Oh... one more thing," Meera stopped to add "You have been invited by the New Age bank for the inauguration of their new building. It would be a good public relations move for you, as the bank has a dynamic woman as their chairman and she personally requested for you to inaugurate it" Meera then added as an afterthought "You have become a sort of symbol for the modern day Indian women." She paused to see if what she had said, brought on any reaction, seeing none she continued "It is on Thursday, do I accept or not?" Tara asked "what else do I have on that day?" Meera quickly replied "Not much, just a few meetings which can be rearranged." "OK, accept their invite, I will check up with Sir later." 'Sir', was the designated name for her husband. With that done and decided, she covered her face with both hands, and when she removed them her cool and controlled mask was back on, and she said "let's go, we are getting late."

CHAPTER 4

Early the next morning, Rohan was the first to get up and get ready. At the breakfast table he told both his wife and mother of Samir's decision, "I am left alone to fight, I am not saying I can't or I won't, I am only saying that I need your full support and trust in whatever I decide to do from now because without that I cannot think of going on." Rohan's mother was the first to reply, "Samir has acted in a manner which does not leave any choice for you Rohan. Your father will be out of the hospital in about fifteen days but Son, I doubt if he will be of much help; so you make the decision and I shall not fight it whatever the consequences." He looked at his wife, Deepa, who also nodded in approval. With that settled it was time to take on the bank. With as much confidence as he could gather, he decided it was time to face Mr. Sharma at the New Age bank.

On his way, he planned his strategy, he decided that this was not the time to fight, I am in no position to fight, he thought to himself, I have to remind him of the good old days and how adversely the bank's decision had affected his father, how he had personally, misled us, I will try to rake up his conscience, he thought, God, I do hope he has some left. Yes, he thought that would be the right approach.

As he was ushered into the office for his appointment, the very first thing that hit him, as soon as he opened the door was the cold blast of the air conditioning. As he stepped in, he was taken aback by the lavishness of the room. The mahogany furniture was complimented by a beige coloured carpet which was so thick that his foot sunk in deep. As he looked at the man sitting behind the table, he could not help but feel a tinge of hate. He knew that this man's deceitful acts towards his father had something, if not much to do with his position of power today, but he masked his feelings in time, just before Mr. Sharma looked up and said a very stiff hello with a equally stiff smile and asked him to sit.

"Congratulations Sir," Rohan offered as he walked up to the table and sat down on the chair offered to him. The banker lifted his eyes from the set of papers he was examining and looked at Rohan, searching for any sign of sarcasm but there was none. He nodded in reply and came down to business immediately. "I sent a letter to your father earlier this week." He paused and continued "Look Rohan, I tried my best but there is only so much that I can do. It is with regret that I tell you that the bank has made a decision." Rohan did not wait for him to continue and interrupted with: "Papa is in hospital. He had a stroke, soon after he read the letter that was sent from your office" Rohan waited for some sort of reaction, "Oh God. How is he????" Exclaimed sharma.

Having got the desired reaction Rohan continued, "Not well Sir but he will make it, that's what the doctors tell us. I just came to put my case to you and the bank, Sir. You had agreed in principal for financing the letter of credit for rice. Based on that, we have already bought one third of the stock, you know that if you do not finance us now we will lose everything. You have to find a way out," and then he added in a small soft voice. "At least for old times' sake."

"I am sorry but the decision was made and I did try my best, as I always do for you but there is a time to let go and this is that time for you, Sharma dismissed the conversation with that to Rohan's utter frustration, he seemed to be indicating, "Over and out with you." Rohan decided instinctively to try a new approach, "You know Mr. Sharma, I can take it and so can my father, but Samir was threatening to complain against you, he has some entries, I am not aware of, maybe you know????" He had Sharma's full attention now, he knew that. Rohan added cautiously, "I know nothing ever comes out of such issues but it can make things very ugly for all of us."

Sharma was suddenly not as comfortable as he had been earlier, "Rohan give me a day and let me see what I can do, I don't promise anything but for old times' sake, I shall see. "Oh…. and Rohan don't do anything hasty that we both may regret later, you more than me, do you understand?"

"Yes Mr. Sharma", I do and I shall wait for your word tomorrow Sir ". As he walked out, he felt that all hope was not lost.

Samir and his mother, were talking to the doctor when Rohan reached the hospital "what did the docter say???" he asked them both and no one in particular, Samir was the first to take notice and replied, "papa is stable now they will keep him in the ICU for two more days and then shift him to the room, how was your day?". Rohan shrugged his shoulders in reply. Their mother bid them to sit beside her and said "Samir's in laws came by, they don't want to postpone the wedding, according to the doctor papa should be home in two weeks time, and the wedding according to schedule is in three weeks, we will not be able to do much, but they do not want to postpone the date. I told them I will let them know after I have talked to all of you including your father, you ask Deepa, also, and then we will decide"

They all sat down for a cup of tea as they discussed the days events, Mrs Uppal was in a sad, soft mood, Rohan was anxious and nervous, only Samir seemed relaxed as they talked.

Early next morning, Rohan received a call from Mr Sharma, he was excited as he kept the receiver down, "what does he say??" asked his wife and mother in unison. "it's not all bad news, it is a mixed baggage of sort, he says, the bank has agreed to finance us, but we have to pay the earlier dues and put up 50 % of the goods, on our own, if we manage to do that the bank will finance the balance quantity of rice", "But how Rohan, how are you going to pay the earlier dues, let alone buying fifty percent of the goods without the banks help, we cant do it we have used up all our finances, this is impossible, what are you thinking" exclaimed Mrs Uppal. Rohan sat down as if to explain, "I am thinking of private finance, it is expensive but will be for a short while and we have something left ma, all is not lost, It is a risk but a calculated risk" he stopped and then added dramatically, "we have the house and we can get finance against it"

This was followed by a stunned silence by both his mother and his wife, who shared none of his enthusiasm.

As Sharma kept his phone down, he had a smug smile on his face they will never be able to pay the dues let alone buy 50 % of the goods, I could have said a direct no, he thought to himself, but, no point in taking a risk, especially at this point with the ongoing investigation. Thank god, he had been more discreet than the Uppals, who were like a open book. They are all so vulnerable he thought and continued on with his work, as far as he was concerned the Uppals were history.

A week had passed, since then Rohan was able to negotiate private finance, against the house. He decided to first put up the balance stock at the ports warehouse in order to reach the 50% mark, as required by the bank, and then pay bank dues so that they can start disbursement of the balance amount. He had to be doubly sure, as the date of shipment was also coming near. It can work, he thought to himself, it has to.

Monday, was an important day for all of them, as Senior Uppal was discharged from the hospital. Samir had been with his father throughout. As the family prepared to leave the hospital, Mr Uppal was shaky but well, he had a slight limp in his right leg and felt that his reflections were slow but the doctor assured him it was the best under the circumstances and with time, it would get better. As soon as they were home, the family sat down together with Mrs Uppal getting the "parsad" she had made early that morning. As they all sat together Samir was the first to speak "papa it has been a very difficult time for all of us, but bhai (brother) has managed things very well, not only has the bank agreed to refinance our company, it is also financing 50 % of the letter of credit for rice ", Rohan coloured a little at the praise, he thought that if

Samir knew the whole truth, he would certainly have other opinions of him.

Senior Uppal spoke his voice sounded tired and feeble, "I have agreed to Samir's wedding date, as was decided earlier, we will have a small wedding and then invite only a few guests for the reception party later, they wanted to share the cost of the reception party, as the wedding is only going to be in the Mandir (temple), I have accepted that" he stopped to catch his breath and then added on "is it allright with all of us?". The silence was considered as consent. "So then all of you run along and prepare for the wedding, we don't have much time." As they all got up to leave, Rohan heard his father call out "Rohan, son, stay back, we have to talk." As everyone else left the room Mr Uppal's voice became stronger and more concerned, "all right, now tell me everything that has happened, I know that snake now, he will not help, so how come?" asked his father referring to Sharma at the bank. Rohan told his father the entire series of event, and continued to tell him that he had arranged finance against the house and not as

Samir put it on his own. He added on "we decided, that we will keep it a secret from Samir, for the time being, as he is likely to object and we don't see any other way out."

His father was thoughtful for a while, and then added on "Samir is ok, he has jumped the ship, but he is safe. That is all I am concerned about, as of now, you Rohan are another story, Son, you have taken a very big step and I still am not sure of the bank, if they can break their word once, they can break it twice, and this time we will have nothing, literally"

"Papa, it is okay, it is a well calculated risk, you see, 40 % of the goods have already reached the warehouse, another four to five days and I will have my 50% stock. Another five days, for the bank to release the funds, we will still be in time for the shipment. We will make it don't worry," he spoke with confidence, "I wish I was as confident as you son, how are the suppliers behaving?" asked his father, "They know nothing of the bank, they have got payment on delivery. As yet, there has been no let down. I am working as you do, I have told them of the shipment date, they are like partners more than suppliers, we have ample stocks, but not many orders this year round, it seems Indonesia, has taken the sheen out of the rice business and we are paying good rate because we are getting a good rate." The discussion lasted well over an hour, after which his father looked exhausted and dismissed the conversation saying "one week and I will be stronger, till then you continue your plan of action, and send Samir for a fifteen days honey moon, we will need to have him out of the way for the time being, go, God help us all".

CHAPTER 5

Monday, was usually a very busy day for the Chief Minister. Taradevi had been to, two meetings, earlier in the day. The first one, had been very taxing on her mind as the grain traders had been agitated for long, and adding to their woes, the rains had been delayed, the monsoon was so bad this year that there was talk of declaring many areas as drought hit. Added to it there had been a steady decline in exports, rice in particular and the millers and traders were fearing, that the worst was yet to hit them. Tara, was well aware of the importance of the support from this section, as they formed an important vote bank, as well as a big hub for raising party funds. Their interest was all important. They were a powerful ally, she had been told time and again.

The second meeting had been fairly easy to handle. The meetings were followed by a visit to nearby village, where the first woman Sarpanch had been elected. By evening, she was ready to call it a day, but her brother had insisted on her presence in some function by a Private MBA institute, recently started in the city.

By the time she reached home, she was totally exhausted nothing could have come between her and her sleep she thought, not even the delicious food of her cook. As she passed the sitting room she saw the all too familiar silhouettes of her husband and brothers, "drinks and gossip session" she thought, just as she was ready to dismiss them, the presence of a complete stranger caught her attention, she had never seen the foreigner ever before, nor was he ever mentioned to her. Her interest in the ongoing conversation was suddenly arisen. As she poised herself in such a way, so as to not be visible to them, yet, she could be in the audible range. As she stood still and heard their conversation she felt a wave of panic go through her. She could not believe what she was hearing. As she stood there listening, she lost count of how long she had been standing there. She slowly, retired to her room, and called for her secretary.

Once they were alone, Taradevi panicked, she was near hysteria "they are planning to disrupt the trade, he has always told me how important an ally the traders are and we have assured them of our full support, this morning itself". Meera spoke, calmly "now you relax, I am sure you heard something wrong, you know how hard you have worked, don't worry. What you are saying is not possible, here take some rest, you are just tired, you will feel better in the morning, I promise". With that she slowly moved out of the room. Despite the sleeping pill, which Tara had taken earlier, sleep evaded her till the wee hours of the morning, finally exhaustion took over and she slept.

Taradevi was awaken by the delicious aroma of tea, as she got up she was surprised to see her husband Raj, he was pouring tea for her, as soon as he saw her wake up, he smiled and invited her for a cup. "what time is it am I late", asked Tara "yes, you are, it is eight thirty, but don't worry, I cancelled all your morning appointments" and then after a pause he added, "we need to talk" he crossed over to her side and handed her a warm cup of tea, and then continued "Meera told me, you overheard our conversation last night and concluded some weird meaning out of it"

She kept her eyes down, yes, I hope I was wrong, is what she said to herself. "look Tara, we are a small party we have been fortunate in the last two elections, but we have to ensure now, more than ever that we manage to win the next one as well". She added immediately, without waiting for him to go on, "how is killing the business going to help us do that?", Raj was on his feet, as if standing and talking will explain things in a better way, "no.. no.. we don't kill any business, we just create hurdles, a lot of them, you see, we are on to the third year....., if the business goes bad for another year, then, in the election year we can be the saviours, fight the centre and blame them, push the trade, remove the hurdles, and, we are home safe for another five years, it's as simple as that". He concluded.

"but what about the them... eh.., you know, a lot of people are going to be wiped out" she was feeling guilty and it showed on her face as well as her tone of voice.

"Casuality of war, don't worry about it, that's the way of life". Was all she got in reply "and the foreigner, what is his interest, who is he?" she continued. "Oh, you see, if the trade goes down, the orders will shift to other markets, now he has some old stocks, which can be mixed and delivered, in an emergency, such things can be overlooked, so if he profits, we profit, understand" he gave her a big smile as if waiting to be applauded for his genius. Tara simply added "can you answer a simple question - how much money is profit???, we are already in profit. where and when is this going to end ", this worked as a booster dose for his anger, and he erupted, with his voice shrill and a few pitches louder. "Look Tara, coming to power is no joke, once you get there, you make powerful enemies, and to fight them you need money, lots of it." then he suddenly, softened up "I have been watching you, you are doing great work, you continue your good deeds, let me handle the business of politics or politics of the business"

"And what about our life, our family, our children??" exclaimed Tara.

"You have a good life, great even, and children are a gift of God, it is the will of God, you just have to accept it" "it was the will of god, which gave me the chance once, but all this," she moved her hands around pointing at everything and nothing in particular "all this, took it away." what is the meaning of that????, "exclaimed her husband" don't go soft on me, I have done a lot for you, and your family as well, this is your life, accept it and thank god for what you have" and with that he walked out the door and slammed it shut behind him. Thank you god, for what!, this, she thought. He is right about one thing though, it is my life, I have to take charge of it. How, but how?????

The start of the fourth week, saw a very nervous Rohan, he had been getting calls from the Egyptian company, who had opened the letter of credit on them. The general manager Procurement, Mr. M.A. Gazzar was especially nervous, Rohan was receiving frantic calls from him, as he was the one who was responsible for placing the order on the Uppal's despite reluctance from the top management of the company.

His reputation of eighteen years in the company was at stake. When he had come to visit six months earlier, he had three more suppliers on the list but had decided to place the order on the Uppals. Now, He was calling at the port's warehouse directly, to ask the status of the goods ready for loading. This was making Rohan very nervous, He had reached the 50 % mark yesterday, as the trucks unloaded, after which he had handed the cheque for the outstanding dues to the bank. Today, was Thursday also Samir's wedding day, also, the day he was to get his sanction letter from the bank.

I have to leave early from the wedding, if I am to keep my appointment with Mr Sharma, was the thought that preoccupied him, while he dressed for the wedding function.

As the family sat through the wedding ceremony, Rohan found it hard to concentrate, his wife was doing a wonderful job of covering up for his lack of involvement, but he could feel her nervous eyes on him from time to time, she had some fasting routine slated for today that would help with everything, or something of the sort, she had told him earlier. I wish it was as simple as that. At eleven thirty Rohan found it too hard, to enact the part of the good host anymore and on the pretext of an emergency he exited. As he walked out the Mandir (temple), the anxious eyes of his mother, father and wife followed him, only Samir was oblivious to his absence.

Taradevi, finished her interview with the magazine, just in time as Meera walked in to remind everyone present that, she had to leave for the inauguration of the New Age bank building. "Meera, I need a cup of tea before the next stop." "Madam", came a matter of fact voice, "we are very late, we were expected around ten thirty and we are leaving only at eleven thirty, it will take us another hour to reach, I shall call ahead, and arrange for tea there itself. "Yes madam" thought Tara to herself "sometimes it's like she is the boss". Tara wanted to say this out loud but she relented instead with a "hmmmm......"

Rohan entered the new "New Age Bank building", Mr Sharma had called him there, as his office had been shifted. Rohan waited eagerly, he almost jumped as his name was announced, he walked in, and as soon as he sat down on the chair that was offered to him, he started to say "here sir, the goods, as decided are at the ports warehouse and dues were paid yesterday itself. Now please, hand me my sanction letter." He sat there beaming, having achieved the near impossible, and they both knew that.

Mr Sharma seemed perfectly at ease, he moved his pen between his hands as he spoke "Rohan, I know we promised you, but it seems that the new policies are not favouring rice exports, and you being new to this field of work, the bank despite having sanctioned, is not willing to take the risk." he simply continued oblivious, to the blizzard of emotions, that his opening line had inflicted inside Rohan. "Since you have paid up all your dues, we can recommend your company, to other banks if you like, but that will take time, you see we have the Chief Minister inaugurating this building today and the staff is all busy."

Rohan had stopped listening, there was a hammering noise in his ears he stood still, his mouth wide open. Sharma continued "Look I am sorry, but its the policy" just as he said that, someone rushed in, shouting "the Chief Minister is here Sir, hurry." Mr Sharma left a shocked Rohan, apologising for the lack of time, he then exited the room, without another glance towards him.

As Tara entered the building, the only thought on her mind was, to get to, that warm cup of tea that was promised to her earlier. The weather had suddenly changed, it was cooler after the unexpected downpour and that added to her want for a nice cup of tea. As she cut the ribbon, in the midst of the flashlights of the cameras and glowing accolades her only thought was "TEA". On the outside she dazzled people with her now, well practiced smile. As they walked into the building she heard a loud noise, not far from her, she saw the security guards running and suddenly a man pushed and ran towards her, the very first thing that hit her about him, was his looks, he was an immensely attractive looking man in his early thirties, she thought well dressed, decent looking, but why was he creating so much commotion. He was about five feet from her when the security guards caught up with him, his eyes blazing, red in colour as he uttered, YOU...., pointing straight at her, you have just killed me and my entire family, why, why do you people do that??? it's you and your policies, damn policies" then he just crashed to the ground weeping like a child. As the chairman present next to her apologised, and the security caught Rohan and pushed him away to the exit, Tara whispered into

Meera's ear, whose expression was of complete disbelief, but Tara, firmly pushed her and ordered "quick I shall be waiting" Her voice left no doubt about who the boss was, this time round.

Sitting in the conference hall she was eager to wrap up the entire photo session and the usual formalities in a matter of minutes. About ten minutes later, Meera summoned in Rohan, to an utterly surprised gathering of eminent bankers. Rohan looked equally baffled. When the lady had summoned the security and ordered to frisk him for arms, he had slowly begun to realise what he had done and the implications of it. Having found nothing, the security led him back to the building, and made him wait about half an hour in isolation and then escorted him to the conference room. He now stood completely stunned as he saw the chief minister quietly sitting in front of him. As she spoke, her voice seemed faint and as if coming from far away, "if you all will excuse me now, I wish to hold another meeting with Mr. Rohan here" In front of her were two sheets of paper, which had complete details about Rohan. One of the many privileges of holding this office she thought, she had already gathered ample information on his background and it was just delivered to her.

"Come Mr. Rohan, please sit down, tea for us Meera" as Rohan sat down dumfounded he could only mutter "I..... I am sorry, I must have been out of my senses, you see the bank took away everything from me, promising me their support and when I asked for their help, they just say policy is not favouring my trade, you see, I think I......." his voice trailed off for the lack of words, he just did not know how to explain himself, simply because there seemed no explanation for what he had done and he knew that now.

As the warm cup of tea was served, Tara leaned back enjoying the delicious aroma and taste of her favourite beverage, and asked politely "why don't you tell me from the start, now that we are here and talking".

Outside the conference room the eminent bankers were getting nervous with each passing moment. Mr

Sharma, was exceptionally, perturbed he was dreading what Rohan might be talking about.

As Rohan gathered the events of the last few weeks, as best as he could, still not believing what had just happened to him, he noticed she was simply scribbling on a piece of paper, whether she was listening to him or not he did not know. At the end of it all Tara spoke, "I would like to help you, but unfortunately I cannot do that for anyone in isolation, it does seem very unfair what has happened to you, but it is not appropriate for me to question the working of the bank, they have their reasons, I will look in to the matter though" With that reply, she got up to leave, and with her stood up her entourage, sitting a few paces from her, they were at attention immediately, as they prepared for her to leave.

As she got up, she offered her hand to Rohan who shook it, but he felt something being pressed into his hand, as she walked away, she smiled and spoke in a low voice "good luck with that" she pointed at his hand and without another glance she walked out of the room, and the entire group with her. As he stood alone in the huge conference hall, he looked down and opened his palm, in it was a neatly folded piece of paper, he looked again at the now empty doorway and back to his hand. Confused, he carefully put the paper in his pocket and walked out the door and out the building, he intended to read it carefully in peace.

CHAPTER 6

As he sat quietly, in the coffee house, a waiter, kept his steaming hot cup of coffee on the table and smiled, Rohan neither saw the coffee nor the smile, he looked at the waiter blankly and waited for him to leave. As soon as he was alone he carefully removed the folded piece of paper from his pocket and began to read its contents, I thought she was working while I talked, but she was actually writing this for me, Rohan thought to himself, as he read the words scribbled on the paper his expression became more and more confused, what the hell is this????. Let me show this to my father, two heads are better than one, he thought, mine specially is not working at the moment, maybe he can make out what this is all about.

That suddenly reminded him of his brother, oh! god, they must be home now, better get there, thought Rohan and quickly put some money on the table and left, his coffee still steaming hot and completely untouched.

As soon as he stepped out of his car, he heard loud voices, laughter and merrymaking in the air. It made him feel strangely nice and relaxed, yet sad. He quickened his pace and as he walked in to the house he was greeted with enquiring, happy faces. 'what happened, where were you?" was the general question, he apologised and joined in the festivities.

Late at night as the last guest left, Rohan called on Samir "you have a flight to catch in the morning, get some rest" and with that a completely exhausted Rohan walked in to his father's room, leaving a much harassed and complaining Deepa to fend for herself.

"Come on in son" boomed his father's voice, as he stepped in, he saw the question in his father's eyes. One week had made him stronger but he did have difficulty moving his right arm. Rohan started speaking as soon as he walked in, "the most amazing thing happened to me today"...... and with that he started telling his father everything that happened right from the moment he entered Mr. Sharma's office, he went on not believing himself, the event's of the day. After he was through he handed the paper to his father, it was a small piece of paper on which was written "S. LAL, CID INVESTIGATOR".

His father seemed even more baffled but he quietly took the paper and said "Rohan you go rest, God knows, you have been through enough, I will think about this, it has to be linked to us, in which way I cannot say now. We will talk about it in the morning. Son, your brother got married today, go and congratulate them." Rohan had no strength to either argue or refute, he simply walked out, with the thought 'TOMORROW is another day'.

It had barely been 5 hrs, since he slept, when he was awakened by his wife, "Samir has to leave for the airport, do you want to drive them down or should he take the driver" she quietly asked him, as if she regretted waking him up him. "Huh......, what???" Rohan didn't quite understand at first but as he looked around, he realised where he was, and what Deepa was talking about. "No wait, we will drop them to the airport, give me ten minutes, no more, you get their luggage and everything loaded, in the SUV we shall take that, it has more space."

As Rohan was walking down the stairway, he saw Samir and his bride say there byes to every one, they all quickly got into the SUV Rohan and Deepa in the front, Samir and his wife in the back. Samir was the first to speak 'bhai (brother) is everything alright, you left the wedding in such a haste, we were wondering..?????"

"Don't worry Samir everything is fine, you two enjoy your holiday, Goa is a beautiful place" As he said that he thought to himself, if I felt half as confident as I am sounding, life would be great.

An hour later, Deepa and Rohan were on their way back home. "don't worry, there is a God, he will set things right" spoke Deepa suddenly. He smiled at her innocence "are you sure there is a God, Deepa, doesn't seem so to me". "OOOH.... don't say such things Rohan." Was all she offered as a reply.

The rest of the journey back home was in complete silence. As they reached home Rohan's mother called out and told him that his father had been asking for him. Rohan ran up the stairs taking two at a time. when he opened the door he saw his father sitting on the chair with the piece of paper in his hand as soon as he saw Rohan he exclaimed "I have contemplated a lot on this, I think we need to find out if there is an investigation going on against Sharma", "investigation???? I did hear about it vaguely let me check up, but even if it is so, what do we gain from it reporting him is not going to help us in anyway, is it??????" Rohan added.

"Lets take one step at a time, ok, if it is true you have to approach this person with care, even if we have to report him we should, I did go along with his demands and see where and when he hit back, look son this is all we have right now, we will cross the bridge when we reach it" Rohan did not look very hopeful, "if this doesn't work we have no choice but to call in the losses,...... and there won't be much left to bank on..." "I do have that in my mind, also, and am also ready for any eventuality son, you are not alone we are all in this together". "now go you have a busy day ahead of you".

As Rohan finished his breakfast he glanced at his mobile and was surprised to see, four missed calls from Egypt, as he drove down to his office he thought they are getting impatient.

Walking into his cabin, he quickly called his confidante in the bank and asked him to make inquiries about Mr. Sharma, he was assured that by evening he will have all the information. With that Rohan started to call the Egyptian company, I have to assure them, that all is well, I have to, can't take chances there. The phone was answered on the second ring itself, they were waiting, he thought "Hello Mr. Gazzar, this is Rohan from India".

A half hour later, Rohan sat alone and thought back on what he had just discussed on the phone. The company it seems was getting very impatient, Gazzar had so far been very cooperative but there seemed to be too much pressure on him, with less than two weeks left for the ship to dock at Kandla port and with only 50 % of the goods in stock, it was difficult to blame him. Rohan had assured him that there was enough time but how would he manage without the bank????

"God I need a miracle............" Rohan called out loud.

Tara walked into her office, and was quite taken aback to see Raj, in deep discussion with Meera. They both kept quiet as she walked in, Meera hurriedly made an excuse and left. "So, what was that all about trying to go solo are we????", mocked Raj, Tara looked completely baffled "what do you mean by that, and what was so important and interesting that the two of you could not wait for me?"

He looked at her accusingly as he spoke in a deep throaty voice, "Tara, what did you do at the bank today, you wanted to have tea with a young boy?, is that it, or are you planning to make your own allies and go solo. WHAT IS IT DAMN IT????," he yelled at her.

"Look Raj, I only acted as a politician, he was in big trouble and I offered him some kind words", Raj seemed nervous, "this is what you have for the last time accept it or......" and with that he walked out the door. Tara sat down trembling, Meera has been reporting to him she realised. As she sat down, she glanced at the paper in front of her, there was a small write up about the inauguration, and an even smaller one about the incident with the rice exporter, it caught her attention as she read through it, she found the writing to be concise and not judgemental at all, it simply put her in a good light as a considerate and patient politician. Still, I hope I never meet that boy again it can only make Raj more angry. Just as she thought that, meera walked back in and spoke in a whisper, "you passed him a note why?? for what???" "what was that is all about?" Tara just looked at her blankly as she spoke "all I wanted was for him to know that the file on the banker was already being investigated and that he should knock on some other door" With that she left the room looking for Raj.

Rohan was suddenly awaken by the shrill ringing of the phone, when did I fall asleep he thought to himself, he quickly picked up the receiver, the conversation lasted about not more than five minutes, as he carefully replaced the receiver, he thought to himself now what???. Rohan immediately dialled home to talk to his father, "hello" the call was answered on the first ring itself. "You were right, he does have an investigation going on and the inspector in charge is S. LAL." There was silence on the other end, it took a good minute for Mr Uppal to answer back, and when he did, his voice was slow and cautious. "Rohan I want you to call up the agency and fix an appointment for tomorrow with him, its only 4: 00 pm as yet, you can still get him, after that...." there was a hesitation in his father's voice, "you come back home straight away". As an afterthought he asked again "son have you seen the newspaper today??" That last question completely threw him off... "what?? no....." "Alright son, fix up for tomorrow and get back home. Things are looking up for you, do it ". With that he heard the line go dead. Newspaper??, he thought, what is he talking about. He quickly put the thought away, he knew he had a lot more important things at hand to do.

The directory service took less than a minute to give him the number, as he started dialling he noticed a sudden quivering in his hands, braced himself for what he had to do and carried on. Four or five rings later the call was answered, by what he presumed as the front desk. "Hello, Yes" "hello, can I talk to inspector S lal?" his voice sounded firm and confident, he wondered how, as he was nowhere close to feeling it. "yes, may I know who is calling and what this is about" came the reply from the other end, "this is Rohan Uppal speaking and it is about a case of his." He was put on hold, it was taking too long, I think they may have forgotten???....., stop, he said to himself I am losing my mind. After about a good three minutes the phone was answered. "Hello" the voice sounded shrill and deep, Good evening sir, I am Rohan Uppal, I needed to talk to you in connection of one of your cases"

"Uppal ji, *Aap ko kaun nahi jaanta* (everyone knows you), you are the hero of the day" Rohan was completely thrown off by the reply and the friendly tone in the voice, "look" continued the voice on the other end "I have to leave for Pune tomorrow, I shall be back in two days. Why don't we meet Monday morning" Rohan wanted to scream, NO.., thats too close for me, but he replied, "Monday sir, I shall call you?", "no, give me your number, I, will call you, we will meet on Monday" there was a firmness in his voice which left no space for negotiation, Rohan gave his numbers and bid good bye to him.

Rohan was completely exhausted as he reached home, his wife was at the door even before he rang the bell, "have you seen the newspaper today??" was the only greeting he got from her," huhh..., what "we were all is waiting for you," called out Deepa.

Rohan stood completely still with the paper in his hand as he read through the article, a brief one, but very prominent. "They actually published this as news, I don't believe this" Was all he could mutter, "that's why lal knew me, I was wondering" his father looked at him and smiled its not all bad son, the only negative I foresee is that the rice millers will hear of this sooner or later and that can be trouble for us, how was our dear Mr. Lal ".

"Oh.. ok, we fixed up for Monday I would have liked it to be earlier than that....., he took my numbers he is going to call me, it seems he would like to meet up somewhere in between, and not his office "his father spoke rather quickly, and then added on, I am leaving for Patiala tomorrow morning I will negotiate and take some credit from the millers, by the time this news gets to them, they should have invested a good amount in credit, that will ensure their support they cannot back out then", "meanwhile you get the ball rolling here, report him and negotiate with the bank again push as much as required, give it all you have got, let's do our best". With that he was dismissed, Just as he turned around, his father added "oh Rohan, got a call from Egypt, Gazzar is coming on Monday, you have to handle him as well, ok son, good night" and with that he turned his lights off. Yes, I have to handle him as well, sure, he thought to himself, I have nothing else to do right. How did life come to this, two months back things were difficult but comfortable, now it is as if I myself have no control over anything anymore. First things first, I need food and sleep, tomorrow we will see.

CHAPTER 7

Friday morning was bright and sunny, as Rohan got up, he realised that it was not so early and he quickly jumped out of bed, as he got ready he felt the house was unusually quiet, before walking down to the kitchen, he decided to check on his father. As he walked in to the room, he saw the bed fully made up and no visible sign of his father, where is he now?? he thought to himself, has he already left for Patiala, he felt nervous, why does that make me feel nervous. He walked towards the kitchen, as soon as he had reached the dining hall, he saw both his mother and wife standing together waiting for him,.... oh no, he thought, I can handle the bank and the rest, god, but not them and that too together, dear lord have you no mercy!!!!!!!.

His smile did not fool either one of them, as he was served breakfast, he felt very much like a goat being fed by the butchers before the final act.........

As the table was cleared, his mother spoke with quite concern "son what is going on, I am terribly confused, your father should be resting right now. what is happening with the bank?, we have been getting calls all day yesterday since that damn article, please tell me..." Rohan did not want to raise her hopes especially when he himself did not feel confident. "Ma, don't worry, we are doing are best, and you only say, do your best and god shall do the rest, right, don't lose your faith now, we need it more now than ever."

At the chief minister's residence, Raj was extremely uncomfortable, nervous even, the incident had confused him, what has she been thinking, did she want to leave him now or was she just trying to make her own allies, that would make her stronger and more difficult to control, I have to stop her now, in her very first step otherwise I do not know where this might end, I do not wish to be the puppet. With that thought he decided to make sure he had all updates on "Rohan Uppal". I have to guard my interest at any cost I have to ensure he does not succeed, I have to set an example.. His own insecurities were making him nervous.

Monday came all too quickly, Rohan got two very important calls in the morning, the first one was from Mr. Lal, who fixed up the meeting for 12 :00 am, sharp, at a little known coffee shop close to his office. The other one was from his father who had managed to base himself in the middle of the millers and with the help of the rice agents, or *dalaals*, as they are more commonly called, managed to strike the deal for payment after delivery to the warehouse at the port, this last piece of information was very exciting, because if all else failed only their support can help achieve the shipment and as such it was imperative to have an upper hand on them. Another, equally important news was that of the Egyptian, he was coming tonight, he would be a problem to handle, but I shall cross the bridge when I reach it. In the meantime I have Mr. Lal to handle. As Rohan walked inside the coffee house, it was not too crowded, six to seven tables were laid out, with only two occupied, as soon as he looked at the one where a tall, broad shouldered man was sitting quietly, he knew he was his man, here we go, was the last thought he had before he walked up to him and introduced himself.

An hour later a very excited Rohan called his father, "you won't believe this, we discussed the business at hand, and he promised me, I will have my sanction letter in two days. He was cooperative and talked to the point, told me what he expected, in cash only." he stopped to catch his breath, and then added "papa, he doesn't ever want to hear or see me again after this transaction, I did not know what to make of it." he felt his heart racing, finally he heard his father say "Rohan, son what has happened in the past six week's makes little sense to me, this, however does".

Sudarshan Lal, waited a good twenty minutes to walk out of the cafe after Rohan left, when he finally did, he seemed very pleased with himself, this a major stroke of luck he was thinking to himself. This was a wonderful opportunity, I had been looking for concrete evidence, these entries were it, I have him now, but no harm making a little profit on the side, might even retire after this. With that thought he moved on, he had to be in the office before lunch.

CHAPTER 8

As Rohan waited at the airport's arrival gate for Gazzar to show up, he started to access his situation, bad, he thought but not impossible. Thirty two trucks had already been inspected and passed, they were on their way to the port, that would make up for seventy percent of the stock, only thirty percent left, if I get my sanction as promised by Wednesday, the millers get paid on time, and the rest can be despatched quickly. Thursday is the big day, the ship docks, we may be a little late one or two days demurrage charged but we can accomplish it, close, very close, but not impossible. Just as he was debating the situation in his mind, he saw the all too familiar face of Mr. Gazzar pop out from behind the glass door of the exit area, he waved and smiled to him, as Gazzar waved back, Rohan felt his smile was not touching his eyes as it usually did, not a good sign he thought to himself.

On the way to the hotel, the discussion was in full swing the Egyptian had not wasted anytime, he wanted an update pronto. Rohan was well prepared for the grilling, he had excuses ready for all the delays and some even sounded very genuine. As they reached the hotel and checked in, Gazzar turned around and spoke in a low firm voice "Rohan my friend, you wait for me in the lounge I shall be back in five minutes, I have some important information to share with you" with that he excused himself and Rohan moved towards the lounge.

The rich and luxurious surroundings of the hotel lobby were completely wasted on him, he was too preoccupied, As he sat in the corner, looking out from the window at the lovely blue water of the pool, he thought to himself, how similar he was to it, all calm and composed on the outside and only a small ripple was needed to stir it up, he had been gambling all this while, then again he thought, that did he really gamble or circumstances just pushed him along. That's what he felt he had been doing moving along accepting changes and doing his best to succeed, but would he????? that remains to be seen.

As if on cue, he saw Gazzar come out of the elevator and move towards him. As they sat facing each other Rohan felt the discomfort of the older man and said "we are on time Mr. Gazzar, we will make it don't worry" "Rohan my friend" said Gazzar in a dangerously calm voice thought Rohan "I have to tell you this, I had proposed to the company, that you get the order as against the other two bidders, but now you see the scenario is very different. Every time we check with the freight forwarder we find a difference between your figures and the one given by him, that does not go down in good light for you, as also for me. As per the last information given to us, you are yet to complete the 5000 Tons required." he stopped to check if he had Rohan's complete attention and then continued "I have to tell you this as the ship is going to dock on Thursday morning and if you cannot complete loading in the assigned time, it will sail on and your order would stand cancelled." Rohan thought a giant rock had just fallen inside the pool and he stuttered and mumbled nonsensical words just as water in the pool would splash out here and there and then finally settle down, at last Rohan caught his emotions and said "we may be late by a day or two you know but we will pay the demurrages, you don't have to, we will, yes we will.... Why cancel then???", Gazzar looked troubled as he spoke again, "if it make you feel any better I am to lose my job, if the ship sails on without being loaded, as your company was shortlisted on my recommendations alone", he took a deep breath and then continued "you see, we open a letter of credit on you, on the basis of a letter of credit opened on us by our buyer, the cargo ship is specified by our buyer and he hires it and sends it for loading to you directly. the Bill of lading is then exchanged with ours on the high seas and we become the exporter" it is quiet a simple way of working in which we never had any problems so far, but if you cannot deliver on time, our date of delivery cannot be kept and as such, a major discrepancy will arise in the payment terms, in this case the company foresees that it is better to cancel than to take the risk." He took another deep breath and then added "Rohan for your sake and mine I hope you keep the date of delivery, my friend". As Rohan sank back in to the luxurious cushions, he had an image of the huge rock falling in to the pool splashing all the water out, he felt quite the same himself, as despite the news he felt he had no more emotions to emote, he quietly looked on, at his friend realising that he was telling the truth.

The news of the movement of trucks, from the rice mill reached Raj late in the evening How could he, now suddenly manage it, was he being helped by Tara?//?, no she had been apologetic and had not entered into any further argument. Anyhow, I cannot let this man succeed.

Then he smiled, a devilish smile as it struck him, how it was possible to do what he intended to do without raising any eyebrows.

Tuesday morning was bright and sunny, as he drove down to the office, the shrill sound of the ring broke his thought process, as he looked at the number being displayed on his phone, a surge of hope erupted inside him, "hello, this is Mr. Sharma; Rohan how are you son???" Rohan was surprised to hear the friendly tone in his voice, he replied "allright sir, what can I do for you???", "oh I have some great news for you, we, at the bank have been assessing your case and have decided to continue full support to our old and loyal partners, such as you, come by my office son and we shall have a cup of tea together and you can collect your sanction papers as well". As Rohan put his phone down, he thought that sounded like a different man there, how quickly they change track.

As soon as he reached his office he called up his father, an hour later he was waiting for Gazzar in the hotel lobby, as he reflected back on his conversation with his father he thought close very close, the news of their financial trouble had reached the agents, but that damage will be taken care of as the trucks start reaching the warehouse today and I can start paying them tomorrow. All the paper work with the bank was being prepared in his office right now, the millers will not start another dispatch before their earlier payments are made. I will make the payments by Wednesday and in the same afternoon the dispatch can start again, We can start the loading onto the ship and the last trucks will reach the port before the loading gets over, yes, we can still make it, I have to tell the good news to Gazzar. As he waited for his friend he felt a calm inside that he had not felt for a long, long time.

CHAPTER 9

As Tara entered the room, Raj was replacing the receiver and smiling to himself. As soon as he saw her enter, he turned and asked her, "so, you heard that eh.." she stood still not realising what he was referring to, and he went on "that tea mate of yours just got lucky suddenly, all his worries vanished, magically. You had a hand in that did you not??" he continued "but some bad luck is going to fall on him again, you see someone just reported at the border that their goods were carrying drugs, so they will be stopped and checked and by the time they are through checking it will be too late." Tara just stared at him shocked, thinking to herself; and that he is doing only to teach me that I am not beyond his control. As he walked out the door he moved slowly savouring his own victory, over what? she thought.

Wednesday morning Rohan got ready bright and early all his efforts were going to succeed today, as he reached his office he was surprised to see a police officer in his cabin. "Yes, how may I help you officer?", the officer moved towards Rohan and offered his hand "sir, I am afraid I have some bad news for you, there has been a movement of trucks from Punjab and Haryana for you company, nothing wrong there, last night we received a call suggesting that the truck's were carrying drugs" Rohan wanted to protest but before he could utter a word the officer continued "this sir, is only a formality, we many a times get such fake calls, sometimes even telling us that arms and ammunition are being smuggled, you company's records have already been checked we think in all probability it is a prank call, but the procedure has to be followed, and your goods will be searched" Rohan did not know how to react to the, news, he simply added "officer, you do what you have to, I shall not interfere in your work at all" Rohan knew whoever was behind this, he had to be very powerful and also extremely shrewd, it is pointless to fight fate, I have been doing so for so long, I thought I was home finally, I thought that I had made it, but no, I have lost, and I have lost everything with this defeat.

Gazzar and Rohan were on to their fourth round of drinks, the news of the earlier events had devastated them both, as they talked and grimaced about how the circumstances had turned against them, they braced themselves for the ultimate doom tomorrow. It was well in to the wee hours of the morning when they said their goodbyes and decided to meet up in the morning and give the news to the Company office in Egypt.

CHAPTER 10

Thursday, morning, Rohan got up with a slight headache and a strong banging sound, as he got up and moved, the banging became more and more loud, it was inside his head or out of it he had no clue till he finally realised that the noise was coming from downstairs, he walked down in his pyjamas to see his mother and wife performing their Pooja. As he walked in his wife smiled and gave some parshad to him. Rohan took the parshad and sat down to talk to both of them. As he explained the unfortunate turn of events, he told them that the ship docked early this morning and there was no way they could make the date of delivery "Gazzar is coming at noon here we intend to call his seniors and let them know, and that's it, we tried very hard but we failed" and with that Rohan walked back to his room.

Gazzer, arrived dot at 12:00 noon, dressed immaculately, as he always did thought Rohan, it is time, as the four of them sat down, Rohan dialled the number and handed the receiver to Gazzar to break the news, "Hello, yes can I talk to the Vice. President" He waited a few seconds and then "yes sir, Gazzar here, I have some really bad news for you, this morning sir, ah....." there was silence Rohan realised that the person on the other end was talking, but as Gazzar's facial expressions changed from sober, apologetic to that of complete and utter shock and disbelief, Rohan thought to himself it can't get any worse or can it, he waited impatiently for the monosyllabic answers of his Egyptian friend to stop, so that he could find out what was going on. The approximately six minutes that the conversation lasted seemed like a life time to everyone present, finally as the receiver was put back on its place, Gazzar spoke his voice seemed troubled and his expression that of disbelief. "It seems that someone reported that our carrier was carrying drugs, and it seems, that they must have been, because, as soon as a notice was sent, the ship just vanished in the early hours of this morning". The Egyptian stopped, weighing his next words, "the buyer is apologetic, and promises to hire another as quickly as possible, and assures all extra payment made due to this delay will be borne by them. I believe, they will be able to negotiate and send another by the end of the coming week".

Rohan, looked at the white faced Egyptian, he looked as if he had just seen a ghost, his otherwise red glowing face looked completely ashen, with a hint of a smile at one corner of his mouth as if he was deciding, whether the news that was just delivered to him was a good part of the bad, or, bad part of the good. The stark similarity of expression on the faces of all involved was that of disbelief, Rohan decided someone had to take charge and as he spoke he heard his voice without actually feeling the words leave his mouth 'it is the will of god... I guess" as soon as he said that he felt, all three set of eyes staring at him, and decide to keep quiet for the rest of the meeting. But the euphoria that was building inside of him, was hard to contain, as he smiled the most fantastic smile, and looked up and said to himself "thank you god, now I know you still exist." As if taking the cue from him everyone on the table started smiling, slyly at first and then openly, they all knew that they had finally won.

Close by in another meeting Chris sat quietly but his displeasure and anger was visible in his actions, how? how did I come to this??? He was saying over and over again in his mind.

The foreigner finally spoke and as he did so he looked directly at Raj, "I have been watching your actions and moving along with you. However, I am forced to say this, that people like you are the biggest hindrance to Companies landing here to bring healthy competition."

He paused and looked around the room "I have learnt from this experience, that I have to first change my way of trusting and following the wrong people, and start fresh by pursuing the system and I start today by closing my operations here with you". He then looked at Tara, it was a warm friendly look of resignation "I did not believe in God but it is when people like you are in places of power and position and their actions that truly lead to miracles." With that he quietly walked out of the conference room.

Tara was the next to leave, as she moved to the door she called back "come on Meera we are getting late and I have a lot to do".

****

Printed in the United States
by Baker & Taylor Publisher Services